Moon Star

By

Jennifer Pickton

Moon Star

Copyright ©2009 by Jennifer Pickton

The right of Jennifer Pickton to be identified as the Author of the Work has been asserted by her in accordance with the Copyright, Designs and patents Act 1988.

First published June 2009
By The Centre of Light,
Letchworth Garden.City.
Herts.UK.

All rights reserved. No part of his book may be reproduced by any mechanical, photographic, or electronic process, or in the form of a phonographic recording; nor may it be stored in a retrieval system, transmitted, or otherwise be copied for public or private use – other than for "fair use" as brief quotations embodied in articles and reviews without prior written permission of the publisher.

The author of this book does not dispense medical advice or prescribe the use of any technique as a form of treatment for physical or medical problems without the advice of a physician, either directly or indirectly. The intent of the author is only to offer information of a general nature to help you in your quest for emotional and spiritual well-being.

In the event you use any of the information in this book for yourself, which is your constitutional right, the author and the publisher assume no responsibility for your actions.

Images from Serif Image Collection and Click Art Classic which are Royalty Free

    Copyright Notice: by Jennifer Pickton.
    All Rights Reserved.

The above information forms this copyright notice © by Jennifer Pickton.

ISBN 144219121X
EAN-13 978-14421912-1-1

        Other Published Books:-

        Call of the Angels
        Holding the Light
        The Stream of Life
        At Heavens Gate
        Mans Bewilderment
        Development and Knowledge
        Insight and Inspiration
        Colour and Messages
        Angels and Healing

Jennifer Pickton

The author is a grandmother and lives in the United Kingdom. She has written a number of books and magazine articles dealing with psychic and spiritual matters and has been inspired to write this short story for her grandchildren so they may come to understand the importance of natural heritage.

Moon Star

Contents

		Page
01	Heritage and Earlier Years	09
02.	The Healing	19
03.	My Mountain Valley Home	25
04.	People and Customs	29
05.	The Big Freeze	39
06.	The Great Invocation	45
07.	The Lakeside Meeting	49
08.	After the Freeze	53
09.	The White Trader	57
10.	Rainbow Aurora	67
11.	The Rainbow Children	75
12.	Post-Script	83
13.	Family Trees	84

Moon Star

Preface

Moon Star

The moon shines an eerie light upon the stream and casts a shadowy reflection upon the water. The moon is a planetary disc that reflects the suns rays, even though the sun does not have direct access to that which it illuminates. The moon is reflective in all its attributes as it looks past the outer covering of forms to look into and reflect the values and meanings with their interpretations. All energy carries attributes and colours within the flow of life power.

A picture is a reflection of a physical manifestation, or it can be a reflection from inner sights and feelings. Both tell stories that can educate and inform. Much is learnt by recording experiences both inwardly and outwardly, so that others who undergo a similar occurrence can understand the meanings more easily.

So much beauty can be relayed by reflective glory. Much that is seen from the inner source is relayed via a sensitive channel, in the pictorial reflections of images of different times, places, and dimensions. Just like a movie, a run of images can make up a story and understandings can be relayed and absorbed.

Moon Star relates her memories, recalling the heritage of her people and the life and times she experienced when amongst her family. She recalls the shamanistic ways taught to her by her grandmother Sky as she in turn instructs her children likewise, so the heritage and understanding of the greater life in spirit may continue through out the centuries.

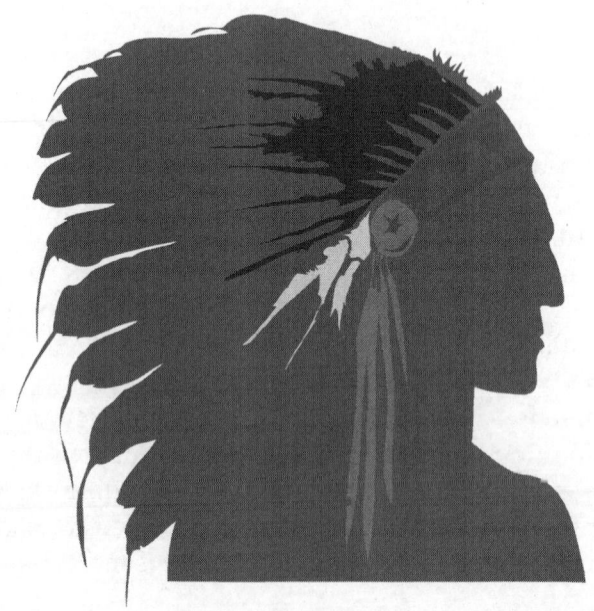

Red Indian Chief

Moon Star

Chapter 1

The Heritage

My Grandmother Sky was the granddaughter of the Chieftain known as Great Thunder Cloud. He had become a legend during his lifetime when he had led an exodus from the south lands, by capturing a herd of fine horses. It was headed by a palomino stallion of magnificent proportions whose fame was locally known as the one who had escaped capture by all who had tried.

To everyone's astonishment Thunder Cloud cornered this stallion and managed to ride him, so the mares of the herd followed wherever they went. When travelling at speed Thunder Cloud and his horses created dust storms in their wake, and the sounds of hooves travelling at speed, became the thunder noise that could be heard some distance away. By travelling north, the arid southlands were left behind.

Moon Star

The parched lands were replaced by a greener landscape of a more temperate climate where water and food was plentiful. Why Great Thunder Cloud left the south, no one really knows, but the story told by his ancestors said he had received a vision. In his vision he was shown this herd of fine horses and told to take them north to start a new life with this herd of prime horseflesh, which would become the nucleus of his wealth and fortune. This came about as foretold in the vision, which enabled him to marry the Princess 'Summers Sky' who was as beautiful as her name implied.

The father of Summers Sky was elderly so he was pleased that his new son-in-law was prosperous and became even more impressed when Thunder Cloud proved to be a good Shamanic leader as his visions were often called upon to steer the tribe forward. When the old man died, it was Thunder Cloud who became chief. His two brothers-in-law were older and had children and grandchildren of their own, so did not want the extra responsibility that came with being chief. Summers Sky had been a child of her father's last marriage, late in life.

Thunder Cloud was also known as the rain maker for he had to perform ceremonies to evoke the nature spirits to bring about the seasons rainfall, at the appropriate times of the year for growth. Because this had been relevant to his life in the south, it was assumed that the same procedure and ceremonies would work, to bring out the sunshine and fine weather when needed. Thunder Cloud spent his life breeding the horses and trading with other groups to add to his prosperity and reputation.

Many of the fine horses that populate the northern plains area, have descended from this original herd, which often produces a replica of the palomino stallion in successive generations. Thunder Cloud had a way with horses for he knew their spirit and his soul seemed strangely linked to the fate of the horses and their welfare.

The gift of visions was strong with Thunder Cloud, but it was Summers Sky who was knowledgeable about the medicinal herbs and had a gentle touch when applying treatments to injuries and hurts. She was much loved and produced eight children that survived to maturity. She had six sons and two daughters. The gifts of vision and healing were inherited by her children but it was more strongly displayed and apparent by one of the sons and one of the daughters in particular.

The eldest son was named Red River because he had been born near the river that passed through the rich red ground of the prairie. When the spring water flowed, the river became red with the earth salts of the land, as the water flowed strongly down from the mountain ranges.

Red River developed the gift of prophecy for when he inhaled the aromatic aromas produced by certain grasses he was able to journey through time and space. He learned the secrets of the future as it applied to his people and the Red Indian nation. This journeying time happened at the monthly moon meetings when the elders linked to the star ancestors and channelled the healing energy for renewal and strength.

The youngest daughter named 'Midnight' was also a visionary with the combined talents for the healing arts. She was a surviving twin and the last child to be born to Thunder Cloud and Summers Sky. It was through her line of inheritance that produced my grandmother Sky who was Midnight's daughter. She was named after Summers Sky her grandmother, and she inherited from her mother and grandmother the gifts of shamanism in great strength, as well as a loving personality. Midnight taught Sky well, as it seemed that the power of visionary sights could be even more powerful, when channelled by a female.

Thus Grandmother Sky became as big a name in our history legend as her Grandfather had. Grandmother Sky became known for the exploits of her trade and profession, as well as her life activities of matchmaker and healer, for it seemed that she had scooped all the gifts and talents from both grandparents as her accomplishments were great and well applauded.

As I, Moon Star became aware of my heritage, I understood more acutely that the gifts I had inherited were a family trait that required preserving and protecting for future generations. I knew it was necessary to maintain the abilities to demonstrate such gifts, as it would ensure that the cultural knowledge and inheritance of our nation's history and ways were preserved for all time.

Throughout the generations, the line of inheritance has been demonstrated by its gifted members and talented individuals, who have shown a wider understanding of their life roles. They have used the information and knowledge relayed from ancestral spirit sources, to maintain the soul heritage of the Red Indian Nation and influence other nations, by the legacy of their legends.

The Early Years

My home valley was located at the bend of a river which flowed through the lower plains of the grasslands. We were industrious peoples as most of us were engaged in either gathering food for the village families or making the baskets and wicker bowls for trading with our neighbours, who exchanged hides of bear, beaver, moose and elk.

Our neighbours lived higher up in mountain country where the forests offered homes to other animals, from which was available in the grasslands. We had horses which we bred for their strength and beauty.

Moon Star

We trained the horses to provide transport for ourselves and goods, when we wished to travel and trade. We also had prairie dogs that we used for hunting. Each family had a pack of dogs as these animals were a valuable treasure when trading for other commodities at the spring or autumn gathering of the tribes.

My sister was named Dawn Mist. We both shared a tepee with our Aunt and Uncle and two male cousins. Our mother, 'Evening Star' had died at the time of giving birth to my sister and our father 'White Feather' had been so distraught that he had left the village and never returned. We were told he had died but we never knew for sure. As adults we were told that he had crossed the mountains at the edges of our known habitation area, to lands unknown and had never returned.

Our Aunt who was called Morning Mist was our mothers older sister and was loving towards us, as she had no daughters of her own, only two sons who were eight and ten years older than us. We, her female kin, made up for the loss of our mother to our aunt, and to our grandmother who was our mothers, mother. Our Grandmother 'Sky' was the Shamanic Healer of our village.

She occupied the tepee next to us, so we spent our time in and out of each others tepee as our needs were met by those of our Aunt and Uncle and Grandmother. Thus we grew to womanhood as part of a wider family, headed by a grandmother who was not only the head of our family, but was also one of the elders of our village, as well as providing other duties as a shamanic healer.

Many members of our tribe visited Grandmothers tepee for medicines, prayers and potions, so she was busy from dawn to dusk. While we were young we lived with our Aunt, and when we were older and were able to help grandmother, we stayed with her.

Moon Star

Morning Mist my aunt, was keen to look after my sister and I when we were small, as she liked babies and small children, for she hoped for more children herself. This never happened as Lone Wolf her husband was always working with the horses or hunting, and seemed to be away a lot.

As soon as Lone Wolfs sons were twelve summers in age, they joined him in his activities and travel, so my aunt Morning Mist, my sister Dawn Mist and I, Moon Star were often the only ones of our family left at home, so we would join Grandmother Sky.

This made practical sense as Morning Mist had not inherited grandmothers shamanic gifts, but understood the need for plants, herbs and minerals to be gathered, to provide the medicinal cures for the natural remedies that Grandmother used. Lone Wolf my uncle was a good provider but he spent most of his time with his horses or dogs, training them to build his team. Our male cousins were some years older than my sister and I, and became occupied with their father's interests outside of the home.

The women stuck together so my aunt with my sister and sometimes myself, helped with the preparation of herbs and medicines that our Grandmother Sky administered and held in store. This is how I became knowledgeable about such matters, as I was surrounded by these activities and the smells of herbs and medicinal plants made me feel warm and safe.

Our two male cousins were not interested in females or anything womanish until they had need of some therapy or medical assistance. Once I had learnt the art of healing, I seemed to attract the people who knew I had a gentle touch. My aunt was happy to provide the ointments and medicine which Grandmother Sky used for the more severe cases, requiring earthly treatments.

Moon Star

I learnt a lot about herbs, spices, roots and grasses. I also had the tendency to daydream when inhaling the aromatic smells and came to understand that this was a time for healing as I could become entranced like Grandmother Sky.

I loved the monthly moon ceremonies when I could communicate with the moon and stars and fill my being with brightness and lightness that made me feel as if I was so special. I felt as if I was lit up like the campfire, as I was full of sparkling flames that danced within me. I felt so full of star energy that I became the moon star of my name and glowed in the darkness for others to see the light of their pathway.

My sister Dawn Mist was like my aunt, Morning Mist while I took after our Grandmother Sky. This explains the roles we choose for our life activities. I think it was expected that I should marry one of the cousins, but as I grew to adulthood, they both found my independent spirit and funny ways somewhat distasteful, as they were afraid of what they could not understand.

That is why they held a healthy respect for their mother, my aunt as she could always threaten them with some magic spell. Although she had not inherited the gifts of her shamanic mother Sky, Morning Mist could mix potions to heal or harm, mend or break. This was powerful medicine so a healthy respect was given to our family members and its kin. Knowledge was power, which the men appreciated and understood, for they did the same to the village women and others with little knowledge, when holding the secrets and special knowledge about the control, management and training of horses and dogs.

My drawings and paintings began to take shape and I incorporated some of my drawings on the baskets and bowls we made for trading. It was to become my trademark. The moon and stars from which I had been named. My sister was one year younger than I, so when we went to the spring gathering of the tribes, I who was named Moon Star was sixteen summers old and Dawn Mist was of fifteen summers. It was at this time that we first encountered Grey Cloud and his friend Two Feathers. Grey Clouds Uncle was 'Long in Tooth', who had brought along his two eldest daughters to the gathering, to find them husbands.

He had booked an audience with Grandmother Sky who was also the chief match maker and regulator. I was helping grandmother in her tepee when the family arrived for their consultation. I was struck by the look of Grey Cloud as he was tall and muscular and had a commanding presence. His Uncle was short in stature and seemed oddly stunted. It seemed funny, for him to have been given the name of 'Long in Tooth'. I learned later that this was a huge joke amongst many of the tribe peoples.

Grey Cloud asked about my drawings as all the goods we traded had my symbols upon them. During the stay of that spring gathering Grey Cloud and I spent quiet moments discussing many topics about our life and families, and the way of spirit and healing. He told me that their small village group, who lived at the foot of the mountains, needed a healer and other industrious people who would be encouraged to join their community, as they were short of able men and women.

I don't remember how it came about exactly, but somehow it was arranged that I would become Grey Clouds wife and his two female cousins would marry my two male cousins. This meant that Grey Clouds female cousins would stay with my family on the plains and I and my sister would go to Grey Clouds family in the mountains.

Grandmother had consulted the spirits and was told this arrangement would be good for all concerned. In a few years both families would be re-united once again, so we should not worry about the separation, as this was our journey of learning and spreading our knowledge to others.

Moon Star

I didn't want to leave my family but I was excited to see the mountains as I had heard stories of this place and its magical properties. My sister would come with me and help to mix herbs like our Aunt did for Grandmother. My sister was given the option to return the following year if she wanted to, after I was married and settled into my new life and home setting.

Dawn Mist had already caught the eye of Two Feathers who was Grey Clouds friend, but he was three years younger than Grey Cloud being eighteen summers. Two Feathers and Dawn Mist would have to wait at least another year before they could marry, so spending time in the village together, would give each of them time to get to know each other better.

As things turned out, Dawn Mist never did return to our Aunts tepee. Eventually both Aunt and Grandmother with both sets of cousins and their families came to join the mountain group as life and circumstances changed. Thus my life started in a new setting that was to become my new home for myself and my children.

My love for Grey Cloud grew and his love for me was never doubted as he always supported me and marvelled at the knowledge I and my sister brought to the community. Within a short while we had every one in the village engaged in some productive activity.

A new energy was felt as my connection to the Great White Spirit grew and my family increased with new babies born in quick succession. A happy few years was spent in prosperity until life altered when the big freeze came to blight our existence and test our resolve.

Moon Star

Chapter 2

<u>The Healing</u>

The man had been brought to the medical tepee suffering from the effects of a bear fight and was delirious. My sister Dawn Mist and I Moon Star set about cleaning the wounds and wrapping his arms and legs with herbal compounds. We ascertained that no bones had been broken but a gash to the chest had become inflamed and this had caused the fever which was now in progress. With our potions and herbs we were able to clean out the wound satisfactory and stitch up the broken skin. Our problem now was to deal with the fever which was raging high.

We fetched flat stones from the stream nearby to use as cool stones as they absorbed the coolness of the stream and by placing them around the patient, much of the heat generated would be extracted and subdued. We burned sage and sandalwood and gave nettle and green grass tea to our patient to drink. We painted his skin with blue dye as this acted as a detoxicant to bring to the surface any poisons that required elimination. We worked some time to bring comfort to our man and then had to sit back and wait for our administrations to take effect.

It was at this time when all the physical treatments had been applied that I would meditate to consult the healing guides of spirit. I knew that if this persons life force was strong he would survive his ordeal, but if the spirit within was weak, he might decide to return to the star spirit realms. Our man was not old so we wanted him to be grounded with the earth energies, so that his inner resolve would be strong and steadfast.

Fevers are often a testing time of the spirit within, so it is vital that every positive step be taken to help, in the process of the inner resolve. We knew this man had suffered disappointment and tragedy in his life for he had lost his first wife and child to the sickness after the big freeze. He had recently been rejected by another female who had caught his eye as a possible mate. Our man had to find reasons to live, for life's own sake and not for any other reason.

My meditations took me into the spirit world where I could see his grandmother and wife holding his young son who had died only recently. They were praying for him to remain upon the earthly plane for his future life possibilities held importance. It was shown to me, that a future role of chief hunter and trader of horses would generate esteem from others within the tribe. The brave would have other children with a widowed wife who would become the love of his life, and reward him with a dynasty of children, all able and knowledgeable in horse welfare and hunting.

The healing spirits worked fast upon the etheric coating of our man to seal off the breaks and tears that the chest injury had brought. In addition the emotional wrapping to his physical form was re-enforced, so that the effect of living the earthly life would fill our patients' heart with energy anew, to revive his life spirit and resolve. The aromatic minted fragrance surrounded us. This brought calmness within the healing tent so my sister and I relaxed while unseen work was taking place.

After a couple of hours our brave was sleeping peacefully. We washed his sweaty body with aromatic oils and scents and wrapped him snugly while he endured the deep healing sleep that follows the elimination of evils and negative debris. We chanted the healing songs to neutralise surrounding negative vibrations and bring the physical and soul bodies into alignment, ready to respond to the self healing powers and restorative vibrations steeped in positive energy and vigour.

The brave spent three days in the healing tent before he recovered sufficiently for his adoptive family to take him into their own tepee, so that they could look after him while he made a full recovery. This man had received a healing of the physical body form to heal his injuries received when hunting bear. He had also received healing of the soul aspects of his being, to mend the hurts of recent life experience from the physical living he had encountered. Thus our man returned to the tribe group a healed and wholesomely restored brave, who was able to start a new phase of living. This brave we had attended and given healing aid to, was named Yellow Feather.

This brave developed and demonstrated a love of early morning rising, to gather the horses together so they could be trained in our ways. He spent hours teaching the young braves the basic understanding of hunting, trapping and fishing. He showed endless patience with those who were not so fast at learning, knowing that kindness and understanding were equally useful attributes, which were required when imparting the necessary skills and knowledge for survival activities. Yellow Feather was to become a welcomed addition to our family in the fullness of time.

The Great White Spirit works in mysterious ways to bring about the intricate avenues by which life experience can manifest and bloom to fullness.

Yellow Feather and young brave

The Teaching:

In the monthly meetings I channel the words of spirit who provide guidance and knowledge:-

I looked around me to see my circle of braves connecting in meditation to the natural spirits around us. As each connects to the energies in mountain, forest and lake, the wind and earth spirits join us, so we may converse in our native way to understand the movements presently afoot.

We who are living upon the earth now are spirit also, so we may merge with the elemental spirits of earth, fire, water and air to become as one with them, and become aware of current movements and circumstances prevailing.

The wind will bring news to the land, forest and lake so all may unite together to bring the energies into a balanced state. By learning how to merge the energies one to the other, the human being can grow and learn much about his habitat and environment. So humans that sit around a circle to commune and expand their awareness, listen to the spirits within your natural habitat and when you do, you will be surprised what you may learn. You are not the only ones with intelligence.

The land spirits hold the ancient records of earth movements, changes and corrections. They know the magnetic links that are displayed as a matrix, like a spider web laid over the surface of the earth. They know the mood of the great seas and oceans as the tides move back and forth.

The sea spirits are fluid and are forever changing with the flow, for water is everywhere. Not only is water contained in the lakes, rivers and oceans, the air contains water, the plants and animals contain water and the land contains water as moisture is within its particles however loose or compact.

The airways are governed by air spirits that drive the winds and currents this way and that. Like the great seas, the currents of the air, follow a system around the globe to encompass it, nurture it, communicate with it and merge with it.

So all spirits have their individual purpose and place but are nevertheless part of a greater system that converges with other systems complimentary to it, so that all systems join with the natural rhythms of nature to make up the earths wholeness of being.

The Great White Spirit overseas these systems as they are the working parts of his body make-up just as you have systems within your human body that make up your whole being. This includes those energy systems which are vital to the form of expression which makes it exactly what it is, and likewise makes you, who you are.

Chapter 3

My Mountain Valley Home

I was Moon Star, daughter of the chief Shamanic Medicine women of our group of native Red Indians. We lived on land which you now know as Canada, within distance of great mountains and forests. This was a fertile land and I lived as an adult, in a valley enclosed by mountains where we saw the seasons come and go.

Wintertime was cold with snow and ice but the stream that ran through our valley kept flowing, even when the thickest snows covered the land. The best fishing was in the big lake which was lower down from our valley home, where the forest animals congregated. This area was safe, for visits from neighbouring groups tended to be made at the large lakeside in spring and autumn time, where exchange of goods and produce was made. The spring gathering was particularly welcomed as renewal of basic items was always sought.

During the winter months the women would make garments, male and female outerwear and headgear and moccasins, water and holding bags, tent panels, blankets and skins, as well as useful items of sowing needles, hand tools, plates and bowls.

Many of these articles were embroidered or painted with decoration, to show the tribe or group which identified the source peoples from which it came. I was always enlisted to design the patterns for paintings or drawings on the tepee panels and also for the decorations on all the garments worn for display or ceremonial purposes. I had learnt my trade when younger by decorating bowls and baskets. We were fortunate for the area of our valley afforded us with the special coloured earth dust, which in the spring months could be gathered and made into the paints, used to colour the drawings.

In addition the men would use these paints for the ceremonial occasions of ancestral gatherings, when the local family groups would gather in celebration of nature's solstice. I was often inspired by nature's patterns in each season, as well as the spirit manifestations of mountain, stream and forest. They showed different aspects of their nature according to the time of year. The animals also brought inspiration, as much of our culture was associated with the indigenous animals of our land. Many of our stories were based on the activities and behaviour of animals, so our children would understand the characteristics of those that were friendly and those that were aggressive and dangerous.

I had four children which grew to adult years, three sons and one daughter. Another son and two daughters were laid to rest beneath the tall pines, as they retuned to the great white spirit during the time of the great freeze and its aftermath.

My eldest son Running Bear was brave and showed little fear. He became a good hunter and a future leader of our people. My second son was Grey Eagle who also was a good hunter and very agile, for he could climb the mountain side with ease to collect the medicinal herbs that grew upon the high rocks in the pure air.

He became knowledgeable about such herbs and was considered a great shamanic healer upon his maturity. My third son was Mountain Fox who was cunning and thoughtful when calculating his moves. He grew to become a great advisor to the nations.

My daughter Rainbow Aurora was the blessing of my life, for she shined with the colours of the rainbow and her goodness of nature was mirrored within her aura and could be seen reflecting the rainbow colours. She had the sight and ear of the Great White Spirit for many came to seek her assistance when troubled in mind and spirit, when overcome with problems of the earthly life.

Moon Star

Chapter 4

People and Customs

    Each day and month my earthly life spirit connected to the heavens as part of our daily and cultural life activities. Each month at the full moon we would hold a ceremony to herald in, the new monthly period of the yearly cycle. There are thirteen moon cycles in each year and each month brought to us, cosmic power and celestial understanding about how the world of earth joined the other celestial bodies and stars, within the universal heavens.

    At the solstice of each season a larger ceremony was held so members of nearby tribes could meet at the lakeside which was lower down from our home valley base. The land around the lake was flat and attracted the wild beasts of the forest, so hunting and gathering was plentiful. This provided happy days for these gatherings, as they usually were of three to four days duration. Fermented corn juice was passed round for the braves of each tribe to drink and it was the reaction to this strong brew which required an extra days sobering.

Moon Star

I always preferred the monthly meetings at home, as we would gather in our family groups and commune with the night sky and stars. This was a time for healing, as the energy flows within the night skies could be tapped, and used to balance any discord within our bodies and minds. Our men were mostly healthy and fit, as the lifestyle of alertness and physical pursuits of hunting and forestry were daily activities. The women worked around the tepees and ventured into safe forest areas to collect herbs and edible plants.

There was natural corn that we gathered, growing on the open land and many other plants mixed in and around the foot of the mountains, which we could gather for food and medicine. On occasions one of our tribe would suffer from tummy problems as they had eaten the wrong root or eaten too much. Often the young braves would experiment with toxic plants, thinking their fathers were being old men when they warned them of the dangers of excess or eating the wrong root.

This is how most youngsters learnt to experience for themselves, when they had not taken note of their elders teachings. The women taught their daughters well, for many family households consisted of two or three generations, where exchange of knowledge was taught during daily living activities. In the evenings the senior members of our tribe would tell stories of the past and retell our heritage stories, so we could pass the knowledge onto our own children when they became of an understandable age.

My husband's mother lived with us as she had been widowed for many years. Grey Cloud was not yet a man when his father had died from an accident. Still Meadow, his mother was a very loving and kind woman who became a second mother to my children. I never had to worry for their welfare, as one of us was always in attendance. We got along very well as we were very similar in nature and she taught me a lot.

I was engaged in the many illustrations of images on the fabrics used in our culture and also training others in the art of drawing from natures colourful life. This activity took time and concentration, so help with the daily living chores was welcomed.

My home was also open to Grey Clouds' sister who was lame, due to the fall from a high cliff which was responsible for their father's accidental death. She had fallen to a ledge and broken her leg which healed crookedly, so her walk was made difficult with a weakened limb.

She worked mainly around the tepee and cooked family meals. She could only walk short journeys to the stream and back. Grey Mist was happy to be helpful and useful as she understood her limitations and would work with her mother to look after the home unit and the younger children and babies. Grey Mist was also good at sewing and was part of the team of women who produced the many embroidered clothes which were highly prized by the other tribes who assembled each spring at the lakeside meeting.

It was usual that the spring meeting was a time of weddings so many ceremonial clothes were produced for these occasions of importance. Our tribal chief was Grey Clouds uncle, his fathers younger brother who had produced only daughters, so Grey Cloud was considered the young leader and second in command, and was treated as such, giving importance to his life skills and attendance at all the male gatherings.

From the age of fourteen summers Grey Cloud assumed the role of family head and that of our Leaders son and heir. Grey Clouds Uncle was called 'Long in Tooth'. I never did understand for a long time why he had this name, for no baby has teeth when it is born, so how could a mother give that name to her son?

I found out that his correct name was Mantuba which means 'Tall Man' but 'Long in Tooth' was short in height, so he became known for his uncanny ability to give great orations, yet when he did so, he did not say much of consequence unless he had to. He was a good showman and liked to dress in his ceremonial robes at the gatherings of his kin.

His two eldest daughters were homely in looks rather than handsome of face or figure, so were married to braves in a neighbouring tribe who happened to be my cousins, and who pledged loyalty to him and his family. This cemented the relationships between the tribal groups, as someone always had a relative living within a neighbouring campsite.

It was through the custom of marriages and transfers, which arose from time to time, due to skill shortages, over population, from other in-balances, and from unforeseen circumstances that the re-allocation of persons occurred. The time of the great freeze was when many children and old relatives died from the extremes of cold or illness, which beset the nations that year, the year of clearing.

It was a time when the great snow mountain spirit breathed her worst, for the family group of ours and our neighbours could not venture far in the terrible blizzards that prevailed. We ran short of food and could not find animals to hunt or earth food to eat, as all was frozen solid and most animals like us, were hiding in their habitats. No one was venturing out, unless they had to.

We had stored dried food and nuts for the winter time as usual, but the cold was so intense that we spent most of our time searching for wood to burn, so we could keep warm. Our supplies were used up very quickly as we were burning fires all day and all night. We even housed two families in one tepee to enable our stocks to last as long as possible. The men and young boys wrapped up in furs to venture upon the snows.

Moon Star

Our men took risks that they would not normally take and we paid a high price when some did not return home. This is how one of my sons died when an avalanche hit the hunting party and buried most of the group.

My husband and his cousin were the leaders and had taken some youngsters with them to search for wood and food. The snow was very thick and it had been difficult to travel in any haste. When the avalanche hit, it covered all the group, but my husband and his cousin were able to uncover themselves and started digging with their hands to find the others.

Our son had been in the middle of the travelling party and he was found with two other young braves frozen in the snow. Only three returned to our village from the hunting party of six. It was a sad time but much worse was to befall us. My daughter 'Still Water' was not yet one summer and the milk from my breast dried up so we had to give her ice water. There was very little corn or fresh berries that could be mashed to a paste so she grew thin and sickly.

When most of us caught the snow fever, it was only the strongest that survived the epidemic. So one day 'Still Water' breathed no more. We had to bury her under rocks as the ground was too hard for digging. The blizzards had stopped by then and all the landscape was covered in white snow which obscured the landmarks we knew.

In due course the ground animals began to venture out to find food so we were able to catch the occasional rabbit and squirrel that was slowed down by the snow and ice. We were fortunate that the stream of our valley was fast moving and even through the time of the big freeze, which froze the edges of our stream as ice, the water continued to find its way through the rocks and boulders on its way to the big lake outside out home valley.

We were not able to have our winter meeting that year, but a lone traveller brought news from the other tribes, that told us they were similarly afflicted by the harsh weather and had also suffered the loss of many members of their tribe community. We had a meeting of our own that year which changed the focus of our small group. The spring that year seemed a long time coming.

I remember spending many nights looking up at the sky and asking the Great White Spirit, why these events should come upon us. I was given the understanding that the Great White Spirit gives us trials, to test the strength of our faith in him, so we must give to the spirit that which he has designated as his, and be thankful of that which has been given to us, in this earthly lifetime.

It was a lesson in the value of life and relationships that the tribe needed, for in the spring a large meeting was held. The elders spent time examining the structure of each group to see if it held all the necessary skills for its efficient workings.

It was at this time that families without a father or provider were paired off with single adult braves who were skilled providers. The braves did not have to take the widows as wives if they did not want to. The widows had free choice to claim a mate. This was a contract arrangement where the widow would be housekeeper and the brave would be provider, so that the young children without a father would have someone to head their family unit. It was a social standing.

Hence many 'uncles' moved between groups. Often the widow was older than the brave allotted to her. This did not matter as often the widow was relatively wealthy as she had her own tepee and equipment from the inheritance of her dead husband. Where there were additional males and females of adult years, family groups claimed their near relations to absorb them into their own family units.

Thus our family group increased by the husbands and families of the two daughters of our leader who were married to my cousins, who had asked if they could return home. In addition, where the husband was head of his extended family his relations came too. Grandmother returned to us and so did Morning Mist who was now a widow as Lone Wolf her husband had died in the epidemic.

Our valley was known as a prosperous place which was well stocked with natural food and minerals and served by the clear water of our valley stream. It was a place where many envied the easy lifestyle we were able to enjoy, as other places outside our valley home were known to be hostile regions.

It was considered by the elders that the groups should unite in larger numbers, so that the proportion of providers was greater. This would ensure that if another bad winter occurred, the provisions could be increased and the able men would be sufficient to keep the group alive and survive the adverse conditions.

This proved to be wise counsel, for a few years after the great freeze we did experience some more harsh winter conditions but were more able to overcome these cold periods, as we had made extra provisions for such events. We were asked to allot extra tepees for storage to keep wood dry during wet and snow periods. We fashioned winter clothes from the furs of all the animals we hunted and used for food.

These garments did not need the elaborate embroidery we used for summer and ceremonial garments. We made stocks of arrows and spears and other hunting equipment to use as was needed and only traded the surplus when all our provisions and needs were met.

About three summers later when my daughter Rainbow Aurora was two summers old, we had a uniting of the tribes at the great lake. At this meeting we had news of invaders from the coastal areas beyond the mountains. This came from the two white traders who lived on the edges of our nation and who had taken wives from the women of our tribe who lived on the plains.

These traders took furs and equipment from the many groups of our tribe to the trading centres at the edges of our nations land borders. They told us of hunting armies that wanted to wipe out our people as the white man wanted our lands for the riches that they contained. I did not understand what riches they referred to as all the riches I knew of, were the plentiful game and richness of free food growing on our land and in our valley home.

We had always been able to roam the land and pick food from the many grasslands and forests that abounded our area habitat. We knew from this meeting that we had to protect out own land from strangers and be careful who we talked to, about where we were and what we were about. Our men were hunters of animals for we did not kill each other, unless in personal combat of some importance to determine justice.

This was a time of great reflection as we needed to consult the Great White Spirit for directions in the future welfare of our tribe and group. It was in this atmosphere that my daughter Rainbow Aurora grew to womanhood. We often consulted the Great White Spirit and she had a natural way with her, that contacted the celestial sources and so much of importance from our ancestors was brought to us through her.

She was revered for all her advice and instructions of a spiritual and practical nature, when referring to the self and personal relationships that impacted upon the individuals within our group.

Moon Star

Rainbow Aurora was 18 summers and did not have any preference for a mate of her own as she was content to cleave to her family and help with the children of others, often acting the teacher and little mother to those who needed her. Many loved her gentle and wise nature and she became very popular with all the family units of our group, charming the old as well as the young men alike.

There were many young braves who took a fancy to have her for wife. She was our only daughter and her father and I had decided she should pick her own mate at the time of her own choosing. We recognised what a special person she was and we were selfish enough to want to keep her with us for as long as possible.

Rainbow Aurora was a princess as she was a direct descendant through my mother, whose own mother, her maternal great grandmother Sky, held the title of Shaman Spirit Woman. It was a pattern of inheritance that the gift of shamanism, with spirit contact or channel, appeared in every generation through the male and female lines, some being more strongly gifted in one aspect or another.

In my case I had inherited the artistic nature and some ability to register the spirit contacts, as well as the gift of understanding herbs and potions, but I had elected to marry early and thus my creative power and energy was channelled into earthly regeneration. It would be much later in my life when I would become a great Shamanic Mother and take my place at the counsel of elders.

It had always been expected that I should become the Shamanic Mother as it had been my grandmother Sky who had last held that position.

While I had many gifts and abilities of those that were above the normal level of understanding, my daughter was someone special who had a direct channel to the ear of the Great White Spirit, and it was to her that many came to talk of their problems or inner feelings.

She had a natural understanding that was part of her nature for while I and others imparted to her all we knew, she repeatedly was able to offer information, knowledge and directions that was so inspired in its simplicity and understanding, that we knew its source was from our celestial forefathers.

Chapter 5

The Big Freeze

The first snows came in blizzards that coated the ground and made the land white. The tall pines were fully coated and a deadly quiet pervaded the area. Only the water running from our stream could be heard in the stillness. All birds and animals seemed to be hiding as this white snow enveloped everything. Our horses and work dogs had huddled together with many of the house dogs sharing our tepees.

A shelter had been erected for some of the horses which provided protection against the worst effects of the blizzards. Horse blankets were distributed amongst the families as each was responsible for at least six horses and as many dogs. We were fortunate that the tall pines flanked the rear of our campsite, as many of the horses became housed beneath this natural overhang, having been let loose to find their own bed and safety.

This was where the snow was not so deep and the overhang of snow upon the branches and leaves provided an upper blanket and roof. At first this seemed a good place for the animals but the snows became so heavy, that many of the branches snapped and the snowfall came tumbling down. As time progressed during this great freeze the snowfalls became our greatest enemy.

The snow blocked paths and flattened all beneath without warning. The mountains disposed of their surplus snows with avalanches cascading the slopes unexpectedly. After the fun was enjoyed by the children with the first snows, the reality of living and surviving within this frozen area had to be faced.

We did not know how long we would be cut off from the valley below, as the paths and trails had been covered and the heavy snows were deceiving in their depths, as we found out to our cost. In previous years the snows would last a short while and quickly disperse as the activity generated from the stream and our habitat area would generate sufficient heat so that it would quickly clear.

This cold spell was particularly severe and continued unabated, so much so, that it seemed that the land had never been so thickly covered. We had to dig our way out of the tepees and carve pathways from one to another. Our firewood was piled high under ice and snow so we had to hack our way to access the wood stock for our needs.

We started to ration the stock of supplies and use one home for cooking and another for drying wet clothes and cloths. We also doubled up on sleeping arrangements. Each day the men went hunting in the forest as very little could be seen venturing upon the grass areas, as it was all covered over. The forest was difficult to navigate because of the snow falls blocking paths and trails, but the smaller animals provided a food source with the occasional boar and deer.

Our men had their hunting skills tested, for never was their responsibility so great, to provide food for our tribe. The snow hare was eagerly sought and tested the quickest of our braves in their skills needed to effect capture. At one time a snow bear was the target of our hunting men, as it too had ventured far in its search for nourishment.

Moon Star

The river was a target for traps to catch badger, beaver, rabbit and goose. This source became a lifeline when the snow piles were at their highest. The ice was everywhere and this made it difficult to move around for both humans and animals alike. We did become inventive by fashioning snow shoes so that walking became easier on the snow, when the weight of a person was more evenly distributed.

Women gathered pine cones and wicker branches to use in the construction of the snow shoes and traps. We lost some of our horses to the freezing temperatures, but this gained us added food and skins to use for garments and carrying bags. The bones became a source of broth for the small children, and the remaining cleaned bone was used to carve tools and useful articles, as well as providing some decorative beads.

The time of the great freeze was hard on all families, as new babies born during this time did not have the best survival conditions as was the case of my own daughter Still Water. She was born during this time and I did not have the nourishment to feed her adequately. Many people became ill with the snow fever which affected the young and old the greatest, for they were the most vulnerable and the most dependant upon others.

This taught our tribe a valuable lesson. About the physical dynamics of the groups abilities and skills, as well as the strength of the spiritual power the group wielded for their own survival and progression. It had become clear that some tribe members had forgotten the power and strength of their forefathers, as they bemoaned their fate. The Great White Spirit came amongst us that winter, for we held our winter meeting in the largest tepee for all those who wanted to attend.

I had become the spiritual leader, who administered the medicines, pills and potions. This was accepted, but I was still young and had not earned the respect of those more senior.

It was when I had also experienced the death of my children that others saw I was not an exception but one of them. I channelled the Great White Spirit who told our group to have faith. For as a group we would once again rise to prominence and become the envy of the nations. We were told we would prosper in ways unimagined. I was told I would have another daughter who would be special and take over the shamanic role of our family.

My other living sons would rise to be noted for their skills and abilities, for each in their way would contribute to the nations heart and fortunes, in a positive and productive manner. The Great White Spirit informed us that this was a testing time to purify the tribe and bring those who were weak in faith and understanding into the fold. This group needed to be unified if it was to become recognised as the premier group and leading star.

At the time of this great discourse our group was relatively small compared to those on the lower plains, so this was a revelation of some importance. More information was given to us on how we were to progress forward and convince the tribes of our ideas.

As always the Great White Spirit is wise, for it was suggested that if we as a group applied ourselves to our crafts, it would be in our trading that we could spread the words to others, so that they may join us and add to our greater skill base.

From this time I became respected by all within the mountain tribe, and like my grandmother Sky, I became the matchmaker also. A year later Rainbow Aurora was born and the light of my life became a reality.

All that had been foretold by the Great White Spirit came to pass with even more events that were beyond anything I could have possibly imagined.

Moon Star

Snow Squirrel

Moon Star

Grandmother Sky

Chapter 6

The Great Invocation.

We were frozen in our mountain retreat and the tempers of every one ran high, for all were apprehensive about their futures. We used the largest of our tepees to accommodate everyone who wanted to attend this winter meeting, but there were some who did not have the faith or understanding and elected to stay with the children during this event.

It was the time of the full moon when the moon itself was high in the sky. The sky was clear as it had stopped snowing some hours before and the stars were visible to the naked eye sparkling quite brightly. I had prepared myself some hours earlier as I felt it necessary to align my energies to that of the moon star of my name.

We sat around the central fire and all present were quiet in expectation. I saw energy swirling around in the atmosphere like the aurora northern lights. I held my hands up to the sky and as I did so this energy stream found its way to me. I felt this energy stream enter my mouth and become absorbed by every cell in my body. This energy transformed me to show my starlight body form – my glowing spirit.

Moon Star

As I had received this starlight energy, by reaching up to the central source of creation, I then paid homage to the Lord of Creation by returning earth energy in thanks, to the cosmos. I did this by opening my arms to the sky and lifting my inner cup of essence to the Great White Spirit. I raised my hands and arms to form a vortex to release this power.

As I did so, a corresponding vortex of energy light was brought to meet my energy exchange, which produced a portal of some magnitude, whereby the healing light and power this energy provided, became a fast flowing stream travelling both ways. I drifted into a trance state and found myself within a circle of Indian braves, each one representing the heads of our twelve tribes that made up the whole Indian nation.

In the centre was our Great Chief who was the head of all nations whom I knew as the Great White Spirit. He stood straight with a full head dress of white feathers upon his head. He wore a white buckskin tunic and trousers decorated with leather strips at the seams and embroidered with symbols of our national heritage as well as the moon, stars and sun of the heavens. The elements were also presented of earth, fire, water and air. There was also an additional fifth symbol of ether to depict the spirit element.

The Great White Spirit was ready to talk and held out his hands. As he did so, the energy flow was seen to pass to the twelve tribal heads represented within this circle I was viewing. Starlight was sent to the twelve tribal heads to aide greater understanding.

I became aware of a White Eagle upon the shoulder of the Great White Spirit. As I focused upon this bird it seemed to impart to me, that it was the messenger who would disperse the words of the Great White Spirit by flying to the far ends of the earth.

As the Great White Spirit spoke, his words became my words, as I spoke his thoughts and directions to the members of my tribe. It would be for our tribal elders to retell these words to the other heads of our nation. We would have this opportunity when the spring arrived and we all assembled at the lakeside, as we did each year for the solstice celebrations. This discourse lasted about one hour and I was told later that all present were spellbound.

Many of those attending had not seen me work in this manner before, as they were not amongst the circle that met for each monthly star healing ceremony. I felt energised but sleepy, so I slept until next day when another gathering was held to formulate plans on the information imparted.

There was a renewed focus on tribe activity and all those whose hearts had been withdrawn, found once again, they were able to open up and became part of an active team. No longer were people apathetic but had renewed hope in the forward thinking of their own futures.

Shortly after this event the snows began to thaw which generated a clearing up programme, so everyone was required to help in the cleaning and preparing for the new work ahead. This is when my daughter Rainbow Aurora was conceived, for everyone was infected by a rejuvenated force.

By the time the spring gathering was held, our tribe had weathered a journey of great proportions and all had grown in personal stature and merit. We held our heads high as our group took centre stage to relate the truths recently given to us.

Moon Star

Rainbow Aurora

Chapter 7

The Lakeside Meeting

The other tribes of our nation were already assembled when our small group finally arrived at the lakeside. My Grandmother Sky was keeping watch and was eager for us to arrive, as she had not seen my family for over six months, since before the big freeze began. She liked the company of her three great grandsons and they in turn sat in wonder, in front of this magnificent women, who was their maternal Great Grandmother and the Shamanic Chief. Grandmother Sky had an enchanting way with children who seemed to become mesmerised in her presence.

This had a calming effect on the high activity levels of the young, as her influence brought the inner nature to the fore, leaving a more thoughtful mind to question and analyse the energetic surroundings. Grandmother was full of miracles so I was never surprised by the uncanny way she had of having an answer for everything.

Our pack horses were laden with the articles we had fashioned for trade, as we had focused on relaying our message to the other groups. We had used symbols in our drawings and paintings and had stamped all the articles for trade with the symbols of our message.

Grandmother Sky was an elder and still active and energetic in all her busy activities. She knew the time had arrived for the amalgamation of the tribes into larger groups, for the future preservation of our life style and wellbeing. It was the convincing of the other elders that was the task ahead of us.

We were well greeted upon our arrival and at first glance the other groups looked as worn out as we were, after the preceding six months, for none of us was without tales to tell about the ravishment and losses within our groups. Tears and joy were the emotions felt, as family members and relations met once again. Our first campsite gathering was one of remembrance for those who had returned to the land of the Star people in the heavens.

There was a great deal of wailing and ranting that continued until early morning. By the following afternoon the elders sat for their first session of deliberation. Grandmother Sky related our messages and instructions for the elders to consider and this they did, for no other group had come up with such extensive plans to put forward for consideration and validation.

A grand plan was formulated so that each section of the nation was as equally apportioned their quota of skilled personnel and families, so that no one tribal unit was disadvantaged more than another. This is how it came about that Grandmother Sky and my Aunt Morning Mist together with her two sons which were my cousins and their families, came to live with us in the mountains.

They came with others to make up the family units, who had been affected by the loss of their main provider. In addition many of the trading goods were pooled so that all groups were provisioned adequately and the surplus was bartered off for individual gain and personal preference. Some of our goods were for ceremonial purposes and these articles were highly prized and valued.

Carvings, drawings, decorated garments and beads were personal valuables and these we had in abundance as our group had spent many hours assigned to this productive work, while we had been confined by the bad weather conditions.

We needed tools of knives and axes, as well as added supplies of corn from the plains area, which was finer than our own. We also took some seeds to plant at the edge of the forest where it was sheltered and protected, and where the soil was rich for growing. If we could grow this corn ourselves, it would make a welcomed change to our diet from what we presently found scattered amongst the long grasses and favoured by the horses.

We used the corn to thicken stews in the cook pot and also to make cornmeal rounds. These corn buns were favoured by those travelling on some distant journey, as it became an instance meal for them. There was no waste with the corn as the stalks made excellent bedding material or was eaten by the horses when green grasses were not available. When braves returned from a hunting trip the natural food gathered was handed to the women for preparation or preserving.

Our farming knowledge was rudimentary at this time but sufficient to supply us with our needs. In later years when my son-in-law had his white father visit us, he was able to show us many ways to improve what we had, and also show us more things we could do to improve our living conditions and welfare. The years brought many outside problems that threatened our way of life in this secluded valley amongst the mountains.

Those that lived here and those that were relatives and close friends guarded the secret location of our habitat well, to preserve our safety and continuing security. This enabled a generation of children to grow to adulthood, to help swell our ranks to make our group strong and resourceful. It was good to be sufficient and to know that as a community we all depended on each other.

Moon Star

We developed good relations with every family as marriage and allotments were made, so eventually each family became an extension of all the others. We were all brothers, sisters, cousins, aunts, and uncles.

My Aunt Morning Mist remarried after five years a widow to a brave who had no family left, as they had all died after the big freeze or from the epidemic. Yellow Feather was originally a brave of the plains and had visited many areas within our nation and had seen many of the other tribes that lived across the lakes and big rivers. He had been one of the braves allotted to a widow as a provider.

My aunt had become a widow on the death of her husband during the epidemic, so when the migration occurred and the allotment of skilled people was distributed, he joined our family unit. At first he was overcome with the closeness of our family and the involvement we had in the healing arts and spiritual health and welfare of our tribal group.

Yellow Feather needed time to get to know us and our ways. He soon saw what a wonderful person my aunt was, when he witnessed her industrious nature and her love of children. She looked after her grandchildren who were my cousin's children and second cousins to my children. She also looked after Grandmother Sky who was now old and getting more frail by the day.

Yellow Feather was seven years younger than Morning Mist but that did not matter at all. He and Morning Mist took in two orphans so they became parents again and found that they had grandchildren of the same ages. This is how my extended family became so large, as the relationships between each family unit became a complex pattern with some interesting variations

Chapter 8

After the Freeze

After the great freeze and the increase in group members, we were fortunate to have within our group, those that were gifted in teaching, both the male and female children. Grey Mist my sister-in-law organised those who could teach the female children and those older males who could possibly be teachers to the young male children.

Some senior members who were grandfathers and those who were not so active, were enlisted into training duties, while grandmothers with some mothers were enlisted to train the young females and small children.

We sometimes worked in shifts so that each family rotated in their duties to the old and young alike. In addition the young men who were in the hunting teams also rotated in their duties, so each hunting party would have experience of hunting or training in the different ways of trapping. There were those who would tame hawks and train wolf dogs to assist in the providing of food for our needs.

Many of the women introduced the teaching of picture drawing to the children and I spent many a happy hour demonstrating my drawing skills and showing the children how the animal spirits looked, when captured in a drawing.

We found some talented artists within our group and soon the enthusiasm was to decorate anything and everything we could. Even the beads for decoration were painted to enhance the beauty and appeal of such adornments. Our ceremonial garments had never been so fine and when we gathered at our lakeside meetings for trade, we became the envy of all other groups as our goods were the finest and the most attractive.

The men were not idle as they kept busy by hunting for our supplies. They also reared the horses and dogs which were bred from our captive stock, as well as the training of both. Each year the stocks were replenished from the native herds within our valley region by the amount used in trade. We always had enough horses for the hunting braves as well as a few to use for travel and carrying purposes.

It was during this time that a certain order became apparent within our society and free time was spent in personal pursuits. The swelling of our ranks meant that many more people needed activities to engage their energies. One such activity was the racing of horses to see who owned the fastest horse and who was the most agile rider.

This activity engaged the energies of the young braves so much so, that each year at the great lake meeting, these horse races would take place and become a major attraction and purpose of attending the lakeside meetings. In addition other pursuits became competitive sports which included the artistry of the bow and arrow.

This was one area of activity that both the young and old could enjoy side by side, combating their wits against each other. Grandfathers were once again in demand to teach the young their battle skills and knowledge, so while in times of peace, these skills could be encouraged to flourish by using them in the sporting activities.

It was felt that this would keep alive and operational, those skills of survival for successive generations. Thus the training of horses and the art of horsemanship became something to be admired as did the art and expertise of using the bow and arrow.

Grey Cloud

Moon Star

MacTavish Clan

Chapter 9

The White Trader

The white trader who had sired White Cloud and Half Moon lived on the edges of our nation at a trading base original set up as a missionary outpost. There was still a pioneering feel about the place as it was constructed of log cabins which better stood the cold climate of winter. There were plenty of logs from the forest that covered the mountainsides and many of the white men were involved in the logging industry. Some of the Indians that lived on the western coastal regions had also taken to the logging profession for they had integrated with the whites after finding themselves cut off from the main tribal groups, after the epidemic which swept the country, killing indiscriminately.

Mr Phillip MacTavish as he was rightly named took up trapping, as he wanted to see more of the country that he had come to and now called home. He joined up with his Irish friend Tom Galway who he had met on the ship voyage, which had sailed from the British Isles. Both young men had left the old country to seek their fortunes in new lands. Tom Galways family had been in forestry and the father of Phillip MacTavish had been a game keeper on a landed estate.

Both young men sought the great outdoors and fancied themselves as grand adventurers. Their journey into and over the mountains took them into Indian country, where they met Standing Bear who had two grown daughters.

MacTavish had a gift for languages so he was able to speak the Indian language very quickly and understood their customs or so he thought. He liked to barter his goods which the Indians seem to appreciate. It was while he was bartering over a pile of beaver and bear hides that he realised the advantageous price he had negotiated also included Standing Bears eldest daughter as wife. She was the one who always smiled at him and made him look at her with her large beckoning eyes. He realised afterwards that Standing Bear was a canny sort of fellow as he had taken advantage of his lack of native Indian custom knowledge to get his 'on the shelf' daughters off his hands.

Mala was twenty summers and considered old in her tribe for being unmarried. Her sister Tula was nineteen summers and should have been married the previous summer, but neither of the sisters wanted to give up the freedom of running their fathers tepee. Mala was obstinate and had considered all her offers of marriage were not good enough and her sister followed her lead.

When Mala first saw the White Trader with yellow hair she was smitten by looks no other had encountered, so she made a deal with her father, that she would marry the white man whom they named Yellow Head if he could arrange it. This Standing Bear did with great success. In one swell move he created a trading link to the outside world by marrying his two eldest daughters to the white men traders.

When Mactavish (Yellow Head) married the eldest daughter Mala and his second daughter Tula married Galway, Standing Bear would have an avenue for trade and gain a wealth of information which would prove very useful to his position as

Tribal Chief. In addition he would get rid of his two interfering and bossy daughters which would give him some peace. Mala and Tula returned with MacTavish and Galway to the Mission township where they were formally married by the Quaker cleric.

Both couples had already gone through an Indian marriage ceremony but both men were from traditional Christian backgrounds and descended from God fearing families and wanted the unions tied up properly. This they felt would secure their connections with the Indian tribe as well as within the white community, for they saw future trade increasing and plenty of profits to be made. Both men were pleased with their new brides as the young women were handsome and pleased to have their own home which they could run as they chose without censure.

At first their husbands were away trapping for months at a time so the two sisters enjoyed the freedom given to them and quickly integrated their friendships with other Indian families engaged in the logging industry. They found cousins and second cousins amongst the community of this trading station who had travelled west after the great clearing time.

Both Mala and Tula produced a child within the first year of marriage. Mala gave birth to Phillip and gave him the Indian name White Cloud to denote his Indian heritage. He was white skinned and had inherited the yellow hair of his father. His features were very much that of Standing Bear his Indian Grandfather. He developed hazel eyes which were a cross between the brown eyes of his mother and the blue eyes of his father.

Mala found it difficult to integrate with the society of white people of her husbands' race as their ways were strange, and even though there were Indians around who were distant relatives, she didn't really like the township as it became too confining, even though its people were Quakers and kind to her. She missed her family and tribe, her other Sisters, Brothers, Aunts and Uncles.

MacTavish was away trapping and trading so Mala was left with only her sister for comfort. Tom Galway who was married to Tula decided to restrict his time away trapping and concentrate on running a trading store taking in furs and other goods from incoming traders and selling them on. This would allow him to stay at home more.

Tula gave birth to a daughter first and then a son. Tom's children were typical in looks of half breed Indians with dark hair, brown eyes and with a slightly lighter skin colour than a full blood. Tula herself died from the influenza when her children were five and six summers. Tom remarried. He hired a half breed from the trading station community as housekeeper, and then took her to wife. She already had a daughter of her own from her first marriage but had another two children by Tom to add to his growing family in the following years.

MacTavish continued trapping as he enjoyed the outdoors and the freedom it gave to him. When it was the yearly meeting for trading, Mala asked to accompany her husband on his trip to her village so she could spend time with her family and so her father could meet his grandson (Phillip) White Cloud. She was expecting another child when they started the long journey over the mountains to her fathers tribe for the trading time.

By the time they arrived it would coincide with the birthing time of her second child. During the journey Mala became unwell and developed some kind of fever or infection. When they arrived at the tribal village she was taken by the women into one of the wigwams to be attended to, as she had become delirious.

MacTavish took his son (Phillip) White Cloud to meet his Grandfather Standing Bear in the Big Central Wigwam.

White Cloud was two summers old when he first met Standing Bear. He stood tall and fearless before his Indian Grandfather who looked at him and smiled. Standing Bear recognised the familiar features of his own face housed in an unfamiliar package of yellow hair and white skin. White Clouds hazel eyes were unusual and attracted a second look. They seemed to laugh at you and bring unexpected mystery.

Here was a child that Standing Bear wanted to bring up as his own for he had to admit that he had missed Mala and her stimulating ways. Perhaps this was just as well as Mala was fighting for her life as she went into labour while in the grip of fever. A girl child was born and named Half Moon as it was at this time she was born. She resembled her mother in looks. Mala lasted another three days before she died of weakness from the birth and the fever.

Another Indian women acted as wet nurse and since Standing Bear made it clear he would look after White Cloud as his grandson and take him into his family, a deal was agreed between Mactavish and Standing Bear, whereby the children would be brought up in the Indian village until they were of school age and would then attend the white mission school.

Mactavish would maintain contact when visiting at trading times and bring information and goods when he could. Thus the pattern of the next few years was established while the children grew. Half Moon grew up in her Aunts home with cousins aplenty. White Cloud was kept close to Standing Bear and learned his ways. It was said that it looked funny to see White Cloud imitating Standing Bear, but no one could deny the kinship between grandfather and grandson.

White Cloud became a miniature copy of his grandfather Standing Bear displaying expressions and mannerisms which were mirror images.

His white father Mactavish was not pleased to see this development, so at the age of eight years, he took White Cloud back to the white encampment over the mountains so he could attend school and learn the white language and the white ways. At first this was a shock to White Cloud as he had been given the freedom of the Indian village and had doting Aunts and Uncles to indulge him, with a Grandfather who was an idol to imitate.

He found his natural father demonstrating an iron will of self discipline he had not seen before. Self sufficiency was a new skill to learn for survival in the open country, together with new customs and a new language to learn, when they arrived at the township. MacTavish hired an Indian woman to keep house called Agnes. She was a grandmother whose own family had been scattered to the winds at the time of the great freeze She only had one half breed daughter as family. She provided a mother figure to Phillip and she was able to talk to him in his Indian language to help him understand what was expected of him in a white society.

Phillip applied himself with the exuberance of youthful adaptability and resolve, and found he had an ability for the white mans words contained in books. Thus he learned about the country from which his father came and other countries over the seas far away. In addition he was taught numbers and how to play a flute. Many who attended class were half breeds and looked more Indian than Phillip.

Once he understood both cultures he became able to deal with men and women of both races, with an ease that held no reservations with either culture. This came about when attending school and standing up for both white and coloured friends at times of disagreements. He was respected for who he was; as the son of MacTavish, as well as for being Standing Bears Grandson. He retuned to the Indian camp for visits and at the age of sixteen summers decided to return to Standing Bears community to be with his sister and take his place within the tribe.

Standing Bear had sired another son after many years of producing daughters, for he had taken another wife during the time White Cloud was away from camp. This new heir to Standing Bear was younger than his grandsons, so it would be some years before this new child was older enough to take his fathers place as chief. The direct line would be honoured, but in the in-between time, it was necessary to have able family members around, to govern and keep order in the tribe.

White Cloud took his place amongst the cousins for he was the eldest grandchild holding a special relationship with his grandfather Standing Bear. White Cloud was aware of his Indian heritage which fulfilled him in many ways, but he also was torn by his heritage to the white race, for he had learnt a great deal from the words in books that had been in the schoolhouse. This had provided him with mental fulfilment. He could travel in his mind to places described far away, and he learnt about other races of peoples who lived like the Indian tribes, who were native peoples of other lands.

White Cloud recognised the intelligence of his white father and the fearlessness he had demonstrated by travelling around the world and entering into a different culture. But he also realised that he needed to feel that he belonged. He needed to be part of a large family again for he had felt isolated, and the only family he had other than his father, was his sister and his Indian Grandfather.

White Cloud was observant to notice that the Indians who had integrated with the white settlers were living unfulfilled lives because they were not fully of one society or another. White Cloud needed to feel part of an Indian family again in order to find out for himself the merits of each culture, now he had reached his adulthood. He decided he wanted to carve out his own life but first see his sister established in a family of her own. He held a great responsibility for her in the absence of their natural father. Standing Bears other two daughters had given him a grandson each who were growing big and strong. Neither bore the great resemblance to their grandfather as did White Cloud, even though he had white skin and yellow hair.

When White Cloud had returned to the camp after finishing his schooling in the white township over the mountains, his hair had been cut short. Now he grew his hair long and plated it like his cousins and adorned his body with the decorative beads and leather braids of his tribe. He soon became integrated once again with his mothers' people and many of the young squaws made eyes at him to indicate they would have him for a husband.

White Cloud knew from talks with his grandfather that the parents of those females were not so keen to have him as a son-in law because of his mixed blood. It was just as well for he did not find any female to his liking as they all seemed to want the status of his being a grandson of Standing Bear.

So White Cloud dismissed females from his mind to concentrate on the hunting and trapping skills he had learnt from both cultures, to contribute to the tribe's wealth for trading purposes. So it came about that when he was twenty three summers, he and his friend Two Feathers joined the trading party to the Big Lake meeting for the spring solstice, where he came to meet his future wife Rainbow Aurora. The great personalities of the tribes which made up the Indian nation were well known by all the tribal units.

Grandmother Sky was revered for her ways and accomplishments. Although they had within the home tribe a number of healers, there was not a shaman of the calibre of Grandmother Sky for she was an elder as well, and through her abilities, held power and magic which had to be witnessed to be believed. White Cloud had heard about Grandmother Sky but did not know if he believed in her magic as he had been in the white mans world where these things were dismissed as unimportant, for the whites also believed in a white spirit and gathered in meetings for regular songs and chanting. The Quakers believed that the God spirit would guide and protect all things and they dismissed any other spirits for this was considered sinful as there was only this one God spirit who could do good and heal.

Half Moon who was White Clouds sister had spent most of her growing years with her mother's Indian people and had no such misgivings about the power of the great white spirit that could relay information about life, and bring messages from the ancestors for comfort and direction.

As soon as she was able, Half Moon booked a meeting with Grandmother Sky for she wanted to know if her choice for a mate was blessed by the Great White Spirit and her future secured with happiness and fulfilment. She also made sure her brother would accompanied her, as she could be quite bossy at times when she thought she knew best and was right.

Thus it proved that her instincts were correct, for as a result of booking that meeting with Grandmother Sky a new chain of events would occur to eventually change the destinies of both tribal groups.

Moon Star

Mother and Child

Chapter 10

Rainbow Aurora.

It was at the summer solstice gathering when Rainbow Aurora was twenty summers that she first took to giving personal consultations. Those who had booked with Grandmother Sky found their appointments transferred to Rainbow Aurora due to the elders pow-wows taking precedence.

The spring time that year had been good and the year looked bright for a good harvest and hunting so the Elders gathered to plan ahead for the best ways to use this anticipated bounty.

The gathering of the tribes that year included those family members who were the half breed offspring, having been sired by the white traders who had taken as wives the daughters of 'Standing Bear'. He was the Great Chief of the tribe living near the plains where buffalo was hunted. He had given his daughters to the white traders to appease the threat of encroachment into our lands. Both daughters had born a son and a daughter. Both had died early, one from childbirth and the other from catching a fever.

Moon Star

The children born were Standing Bears grandchildren and he insisted that they spend at least six months of each year with their mothers people. In the case of the yellow head trader, whose wife had died when his children were small, he had allowed both his son and daughter to be brought up by his wife's family, choosing to visit at those times when the seasons allowed.

Hence all the half cast children occupied Standing Bears tepee as part of his extended family at this meeting. The son of the yellow head trader was fair of skin and had inherited his fathers light hair colour. In all other respects he looked like a carbon copy of his grandfather Standing Bear.

He was a fine figure of a young man with broad shoulders and a muscular body. He was taller than his grandfather by half a head and was as strong and as fearless as the best full blooded brave. His eyes were hazel unlike his mothers who had brown eyes and his father who had blue eyes. His sister was darker and bore little resemblance to her father, taking all the looks from her mother who had been some beauty. Half Moon was the same age as my daughter Rainbow Aurora while her brother was two or three years older.

This light haired brave was looked upon with favour by many young women looking for a husband, but he ignored them all, for he was well aware he was different and knew that there was an undercurrent of non-acceptance. He was not always desired by the parents of those families looking for a son–in–law because of his heritage, even though he was Standing Bears grandson. He was however revered by his fellow braves and they accepted him without a problem.

At the campfire the families assembled and introductions were made. The young people always socialised while their elders were doing the same.

Many people had heard of the gifts and abilities of our family so Rainbow Aurora was in demand to give consultations to those who would seek their future directions. Grandmother Sky had delegated the bulk of her personal consultations to her grand daughter as she had the ceremonial duties to attend to. Rainbow Aurora was approached by Half Moon (Elizabeth) the sister to the white brave (Phillip) to give a consultation to herself and her brother who was known to us as White Cloud.

Half Moon was easy to read as she was as open and carefree as her mother had been. She had a loving heart and was quite at home with her mothers family, having forged a strong link with her aunts, uncles and ethnic cousins. She already had her eye on a brave for a husband who reciprocated her interest and was her second cousin. She wanted to know if she would have a good future and if the spirits were pleased with her choice of mate. This was all confirmed with ease as she would be integrated into the tribal customs of our nation without any problems arising.

White Cloud was another story. He did not want a consultation with Rainbow Aurora nor had he asked for one. It had been his sister who had made the arrangements. White Cloud did not like unrelated females and was not looking for any involvement. He did not believe in the spirits as his sister did. He held the view that he could make his own destiny and by his own hand he would live or die.

He honoured his grandfather but he also had strong connections to his natural father which he found he could not break. Because he had been taken to the white mans settlement when young and had seen his father's people at close hand, White Cloud had witnessed the white people becoming settlers, and it was these settlers who built homesteads in which to bring up their families and work the land, by farming and keeping horses that had left a lasting impression upon him.

White Cloud loved horses and the freedom that outdoors gave to him. He was torn by two cultures and felt at times he did not fit with either one. He had made a choice to live with his grandfather because of his sister and her future, but he did not find any of the tribe women pleasing to him, as they all seem to have false hearts.

I think he was shaken when he first met Rainbow Aurora as she did not show any personal interest in him at first, but she was mesmerised by his eyes as she could see into them - right down to his soul. What she saw frightened her, for she had met the man whose life would be joined to hers and together they would lead the tribe forward into the next generation.

White Cloud would play a vital part in the future meetings of the tribes, as the white man and his ways came ever nearer and impinged upon our culture. What she saw were her own children journeying across the mountains to be schooled by the whites. She saw her husband being a link between the cultures. Her father-in-law would also play a part in forging new relations between the differing peoples and would set up meeting places for trade and discourse. What would be agreed would bind all the tribes of this area and designate future safe hunting grounds.

Rainbow Aurora knew that this would not come about easily and did not know if White Cloud found her pleasing. Rainbow Aurora could not give White Cloud the consultation he sought as both of them sat wide eyed looking at each other, drinking up the knowledge that only those involved can give to each other. The knowing was instant so White Cloud went to speak to his grandfather who in turn summoned Grey Cloud and I, Moon Star to his tepee. This was unusual so there was speculation by all, as to what was taking place. Standing Bear did not know that we had left the decision of choosing a mate to Rainbow Aurora herself.

Moon Star

Grey Cloud and I knew that when Rainbow Aurora made her choice of mate, it would be someone who was destined to make a difference in some way, as Rainbow Aurora was so special herself, only another who was special like her, could match her in union.

We had to tell Standing Bear that Rainbow Aurora was the one from whom he must obtain agreement, so Rainbow Aurora was summoned to this meeting also. She seemed to know what it was about and showed no fear or agitation. She heard Standing Bear offer his grandson as a husband to her and asked if she would accept him. Rainbow Aurora smiled and said she would have him if he accepted certain conditions to the union.

Rainbow Aurora stated that her husband would have to live in her home valley as it was protected by natural borders and knowing what she knew about future events effecting the tribes in the other areas of their nations habitat, she must protect her family at all costs. This condition was not negotiable. We were all astounded, as it was custom for a wife to go to the husbands family on marriage.

She also insisted that White Clouds father must join them each year to maintain contact and provide outside information as necessary as he did for Standing Bear. We were even more astounded as the white man was not favoured by anyone, only tolerated as was necessary. Grey Cloud and I knew that if Rainbow Aurora wished for this to come about, she must have good reasons.

We knew that she would not risk the security of our family and group so we accepted that we must concur with her conditions. If she had chosen White Cloud to become her husband and our son-in-law, it was after all her choice, to be respected. This was a choice which we had given to her, in recognition of her gifts and wisdom.

Moon Star

At the time I did not fully understand why her choice had to be this half-breed white Indian, but I grew to understand all, as the years passed and the future unfolded.

Rainbow Aurora was always the wise one, the beautiful one. She lit up the lives of all she loved and cared for. White Cloud glowed in appreciation of this woman who became his wife, and discovered he had at last found his home. Not only had he found his life mate, but his new homeland was a welcomed attraction.

Rainbow Aurora set about introducing him to spirit ways and soon he discovered he too had understanding of the great white spirit who governed all things in the earthly life. Indeed he was so grateful to the Great White Spirit for giving him Rainbow Aurora that he never questioned or doubted spirit existence again. White Cloud took his place with his three brother-in-laws who were all as special as he, and had prime standing in our mountain valley community. White Cloud found at last, he belonged in this new homeland and with its people.

Our Group had enlarged over the years but our valley was large and productive. With the help of White Cloud and his fathers influence, log cabins were constructed for winter housing and further storage. We used the tepees for spring and summertime and also while travelling to the lakeside meetings. At other times we came to live in the wood cabins located at the foot of Snow Mountain.

This was higher up the valley where our stream became smaller but was much faster in its flow. It was nearer to the thicker forest areas where more animals could be found and traps could be laid. We also found some large caves in which were further sources of clear water and where the coloured earth was found to give us paints for our artistry.

This was a time of new beginnings with new influences and greater co-operation between the group members. It was a time of closeness between families and the welding of dependences upon one and another. It was acknowledged that tighter control of group activities was required so that the valley group could survive and prosper, now and in the future years ahead.

Two Feathers

Moon Star

Chapter 11

The Rainbow Children

Rainbow Aurora settled down to married life with White Cloud and in two years produced two sons. The first was known as Pip as the name Phillip was given to him, as it was the same name as White Clouds white name. He was light of skin with dark hair and blue eyes inherited from his white grandfather. He also had inherited the finer features of his white grandfather together with his interest in trapping and hunting and the taming of birds.

His frame was inherited from his father White Cloud as was his love for horses and the outdoors. Pip grew to be tall and muscular. He also inherited the interest in shamanic drumming and joined in with the monthly spiritual rituals which were from his mothers Indian heritage. He inherited the shamanic gift of sensing and far seeing or remote viewing which was a valuable asset when hunting and linking back to base when on travels. He was a deep thinker and had an alert enquiring mind. It was said he had a wise head on young shoulders. He also had a mind that wanted to know as much as possible.

The second son was born eleven months after the first. The moment he was born it became obvious he would be a large influence as he yelled heartedly. What was shocking was the hair on his head. It was like red fire so he was named Redman. His white name was (Richard) but known as Redman as the name was acceptable in both cultures. He would grow to become tall and muscular like White Cloud his father. His skin colour was light golden and his eyes were amber so with his deep auburn fire hair as an adult, the name of Redman was very appropriate and descriptive of his appearance. The brothers grew to be about the same size as each other, and as children were inseparable.

Hunting and fishing were their favourite activity and both loved listening to the stories from both grand parents about their history heritage as both became mesmerised by the colourful stores that each culture offered. They found out from their White Grandfather who visited each year, that his heritage came from Ireland and Scotland, which were lands over the big seas far away. The hair colouring of Red, Yellow and Black were characteristic of the white Grand Fathers Scottish race.

The White Great Grandfather was a McTavish from Scotland and was one of two brothers, one yellow haired and one red haired. The yellow haired trapper, White Clouds father was descended from the Red haired brother who had been a ferocious warrior of the Celts, a race of peoples known for their natural understanding of earth energies and natural insight to those nature spirits which inhabit every land.

The White Grandfather told stories of little people who inhabited the glens, lakes and rocks and had magical powers. He also told stories of his own travels over land and sea from the other side of the world where people lived in towns and the countryside, in houses built on streets paved flat for walking upon.

He told his story of travelling in a ship to this land of Canada and joining a Quaker mission community situated over the other side of our mountain range which gave access to the sea coast. His also told the story of how he had become a trapper and trader and met Standing Bears Daughter who had become his wife. His daughter, White Clouds sister Half Moon and her family still lived with Standing Bears tribe on the plains. Her children were cousins to our children.

Redman also took to shamanic drumming and pipe playing to evoke the Spirit energies which were very strong within him. He understood more acutely his mother's ability to converse with the Great White Spirit and the need for conversations to the tribe to keep the faith for future prosperity.

He cleaved more to his parents Indian heritage as the inner vision was clear within him. He did not dismiss his white heritage as he found that his gift for drawing came from his mothers people as well as his white grandfathers people, as his white great grandmother Mary Ennis from Ireland had been an accomplish artist. He was able to draw pictures of the hills and streams and places that were in other lands, by the images produced from the memories of his white grandfather, when he spoke about his childhood and younger days in both Scotland and Ireland before his journey to Canada on a sea vessel.

By the time Redman was two years old and Pip was three years old, they were joined by their twin sisters Morning Glow and Golden Dawn. Twins were not unheard of but were very rare as there were no other twins in our group. I was reminded that Grandmother Sky had been a twin but her sister had died at birth so it had been forgotten that twins were a family trait. The twins were like their mother Rainbow Aurora in features, inheriting the heart shaped face and dainty bone structure, but their colouring differed from each other.

Morning Glow was given the white name of Mary the name of her white Great Grandmother and Golden Dawn was given the white name of Gloria her white grandfathers sister. Morning Glow (Mary) was the eldest and had inherited the white skin of her father and white grandfather. She had also inherited White Clouds hazel eyes. Her hair was fair as a child but became a rich golden brown as an adult. She could pass as a white person very easily for she would not look out of place.

Her sister Golden Dawn (Gloria) was identical in facial features but had inherited the blue eyes of her white grandfather. In addition her hair was bright yellow which changed to a pure gold in adulthood. Golden Dawns skin colour was the same as her brother Redmans, a light golden colour, so when she stood as an adult she became known as the golden girl, with the sky blue eyes that penetrated to the depths of your soul.

She too could have been integrated into white society if she had wanted, but her nature was too volatile to be held in check by any regulatory society. She needed freedom to express her gifts and her nature, and that could only be accomplished by having the freedom to operate in the Indian cultural framework. Both girls showed that they too had inherited the shamanistic gifts for one would instantly know what the other was thinking and doing.

They took to healing, herbs and medicine without showing the slightest reluctance and Golden Dawn showed a particular tendency to become another Shamanic Medicine Woman. Morning Glow like Pip her brother had the gift of distant viewing as well as the skills of mixing the compounds for medical purposes. Morning Glow was quieter than her sister Golden Dawn even though she was the eldest of the two girls; it was Golden Dawn who tended to lead.

Another son was born 3 years after the girls. Golden Bear had golden skin with dark hair and amber eyes.

He was a little sunshine of a boy when small and grew to be the shadow of Redman his older brother, as he too had inherited the shamanic gifts with force. He drew the sunshine to him and everyone loved him as they did his mother for he had inherited Rainbow Auroras beautiful nature to the full. His physical stature resembled his father White Cloud, and while there was little of the white blood to show in his appearance, he had the gift of language and speech which manifested in addressing both cultures, when necessary and required.

He became an orator like 'Long in Tooth' his Indian Great, Great Uncle, who had been leader of the tribe three generation before and was known in the history recall, as the one who initiated the great deliberation to all the tribes. In Golden Bears life he would have dealings with the whites through his white grandfather and elder brother Pip, and come to represent the tribe on land matters. He would be the liaison officer who could speak for both cultures with ease and surety.

There was powerful medicine with Golden Bear and one day it would be needed when the heads of all the big nations met, to deliberate native boundaries and land rights, thereby fulfilling the prophecy of the Great White Spirit who foretold such happenings, at the time of the great clearing at the winter solstice meeting, during the time of the great freeze some fifty years earlier.

Present Day

As the years rolled on and the grandchildren grew to maturity the world changed considerably. The Indians who elected to remain on the plains were moved to reservations as the white man encroached upon our territory. Here in our land known as Canada the rule of law was established by soldiers in red jackets who brought the law of the White Queen who was their nations ruler.

Moon Star

This white woman Queen was respected as her justice was fair and honourable and it was said to be applicable to all peoples irrespective of natural race or creed. At first this rule which the white soldiers brought was viewed with suspicion, but gradually as the barriers between the peoples of different races became more tolerant, the truce between the many different groups of peoples became one of acceptance.

Our valley home in the mountains provided a safe haven for a long time, as the people of our tribal group became recluses, so that it was left an unexplored territory by the white man until a formal mapping of the country took place.

When this occurred it involved representations of each ethnic group claiming their traditional home ground, and negotiating boundaries and parameters of land, lakes and rivers. In the fullness of time it can be seen that the children of Rainbow Aurora were the key personnel who were responsible for negotiating the modern framework of developments we see in present times.

I Moon Star lived to see my great, great, grand children. Through my rainbow grandchildren and their children the influence of our culture was spread wider than even I could have envisaged. Those who adopted the white culture learned about other peoples of the world and one great grandson became an explorer and circumnavigated the planet. He revisited the Scottish isles and made contact with relatives of the Mactavish clan. He became well known within the local community and a valued member and contributor to the British Natural History Museum, with his exploits of discovery documented for world history.

Another great grandchild became a member of the ruling government of Canada specialising in ethnic sociology and to this day his family has contacts in the department affecting national ethnic population and habitats.

Through my grand children Pip and Mary the avenues of Education and local Council rulings became prominent and developed into key activities for successive generations.

Redman and Golden Dawn followed by Golden Bear held the shamanic heritage like a shinning star, during the many years of great change affecting our peoples. They taught others to understand the mysteries of the Great Spirit and to hold pure in their hearts the teachings of the Star people.

Through their children and their offspring the culture has been preserved. Many times the power has been weakened by the prevailing circumstances but has not diminished or been extinguished.

In the now times the presence of the Great White Spirit can be felt again rising to prominence. Visitors from all nations are now interested in our tribe and its cultural heritage and many come to see for themselves the way we lived within our mountain homeland.

The snow mountain stands proudly, sending its protection to our mountain habitat, so our souls can feel that unity of tribal community, as we again assemble for the spring solstice meeting. A new era begins, the power is rising and life takes on a new glow............

The End

Moon Star

Chapter 12.
Post ~ Script

Present Time

From the research undertaken it is believed that the tribal grounds depicted, are the traditional homeland of the Carrier people known as the Yekooche nation, who inhabit to this day the mountain regions of the upper Rockies within the Canadian Country area of British Columbia, around the northwest area, where Nancut Creek drains Cunningham Lake into the Stuart Lake.

During the first part of the 20th Century when the regions were opened up for extensive forestry and mining activities, the children of native peoples were taken into the white schools away from their families in the border communities. This had a devastating effect on native families and produced a dysfunctional effect within the native tribes. In the present times a redress of this misfortunate practice is current Canadian policy, so a revival of native cultural arts and crafts are being re-taught.

The establishment of schools which also act as the tribal meeting houses are being provided by government funding as part of forward planning for the native Red Indian tribes' future. Even the language and local dialects are taught to those of born indigenous heritage. Arts and Crafts are seeing a revival for the tourists both local and worldwide, who are anxious to view the habitat and workings of such peoples of ancient origins. As the world enters into a New Age of understanding, the practices of all thing shamanic is also being revived, and it is found that in many old cultures, the long ago practices of shamanism are identical to each other, in their connections to spirit, nature and natural life formations.

Chapter 13.

Family Trees

1. **Native Female Line**
2. **Native Male Line**
3. **White Heritage Line**

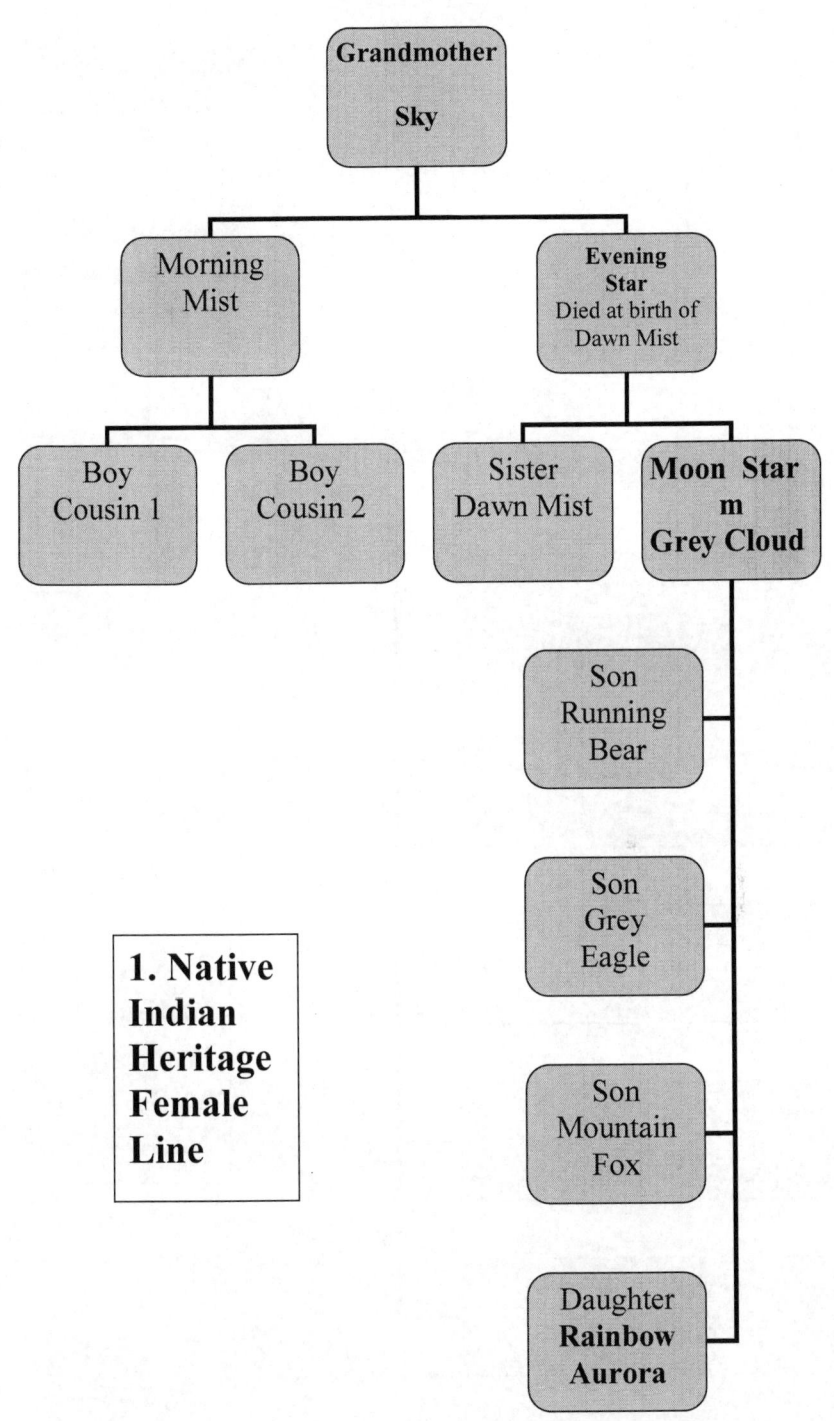

Moon Star

```
                    ┌─────────────────┐
                    │  Grandmother    │
                    │      Sky        │
                    └────────┬────────┘
                    ┌────────┴────────┐
            ┌───────┴──────┐   ┌──────┴───────┐
            │   Morning    │   │  Evening Star│
            │     Mist     │   │ Died at birth│
            │              │   │ of Dawn Mist │
            └──┬────────┬──┘   └──┬────────┬──┘
         ┌────┴─┐   ┌──┴───┐  ┌──┴──┐  ┌──┴──────┐
         │ Boy  │   │ Boy  │  │Sister│ │Moon Star│
         │Cousin│   │Cousin│  │ Dawn │ │    m    │
         │  1   │   │  2   │  │ Mist │ │Grey Cloud│
         └──────┘   └──────┘  └──────┘ └────┬────┘
```

- Son Running Bear
- Son Grey Eagle
- Son Mountain Fox
- Daughter **Rainbow Aurora**

1. Native Indian Heritage Female Line

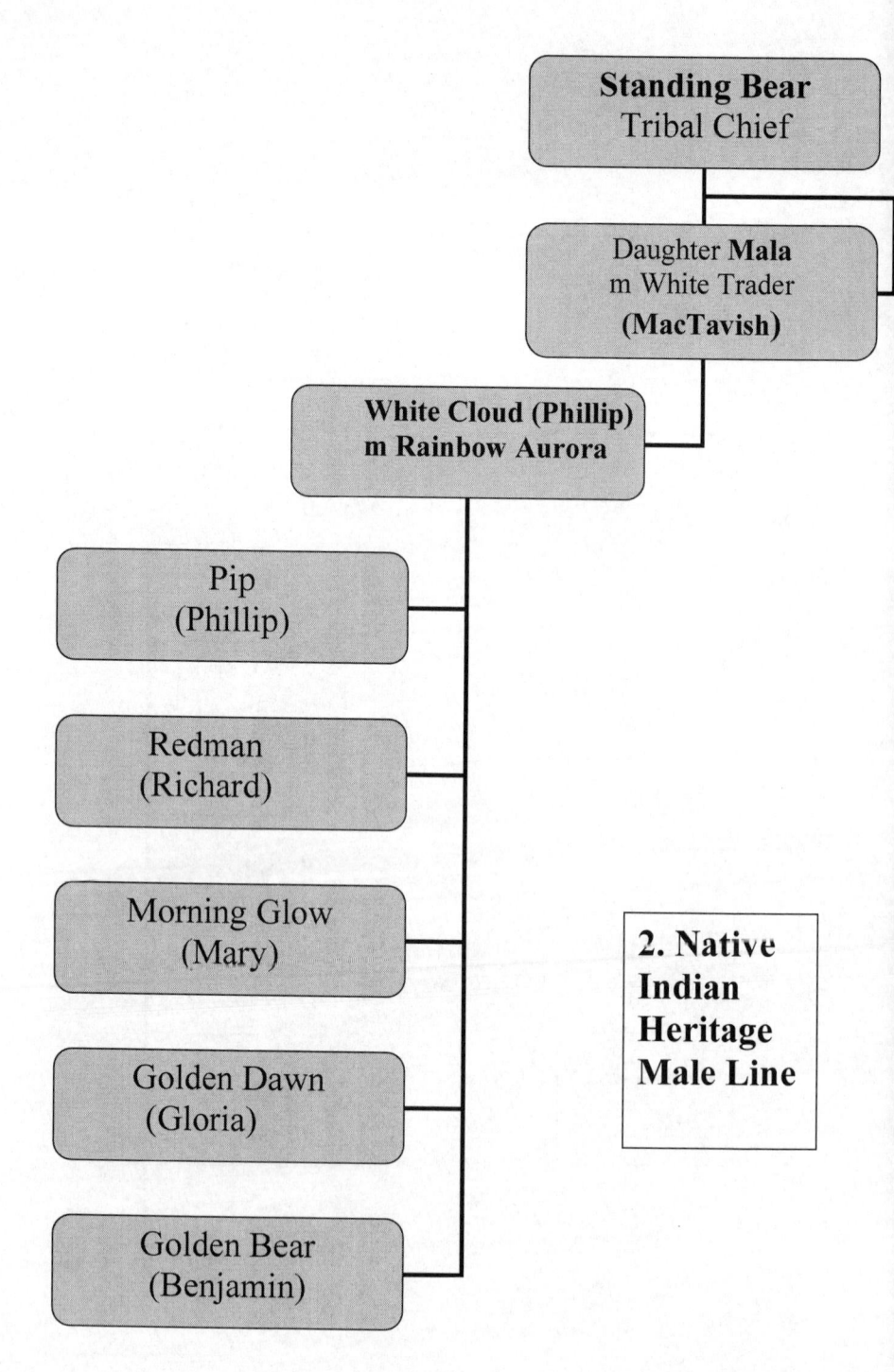

Moon Star

- **Standing Bear** Tribal Chief
  - Daughter **Mala** m White Trader **(MacTavish)**
    - **White Cloud (Phillip) m Rainbow Aurora**
      - Pip (Phillip)
      - Redman (Richard)
      - Morning Glow (Mary)
      - Golden Dawn (Gloria)
      - Golden Bear (Benjamin)

2. Native Indian Heritage Male Line

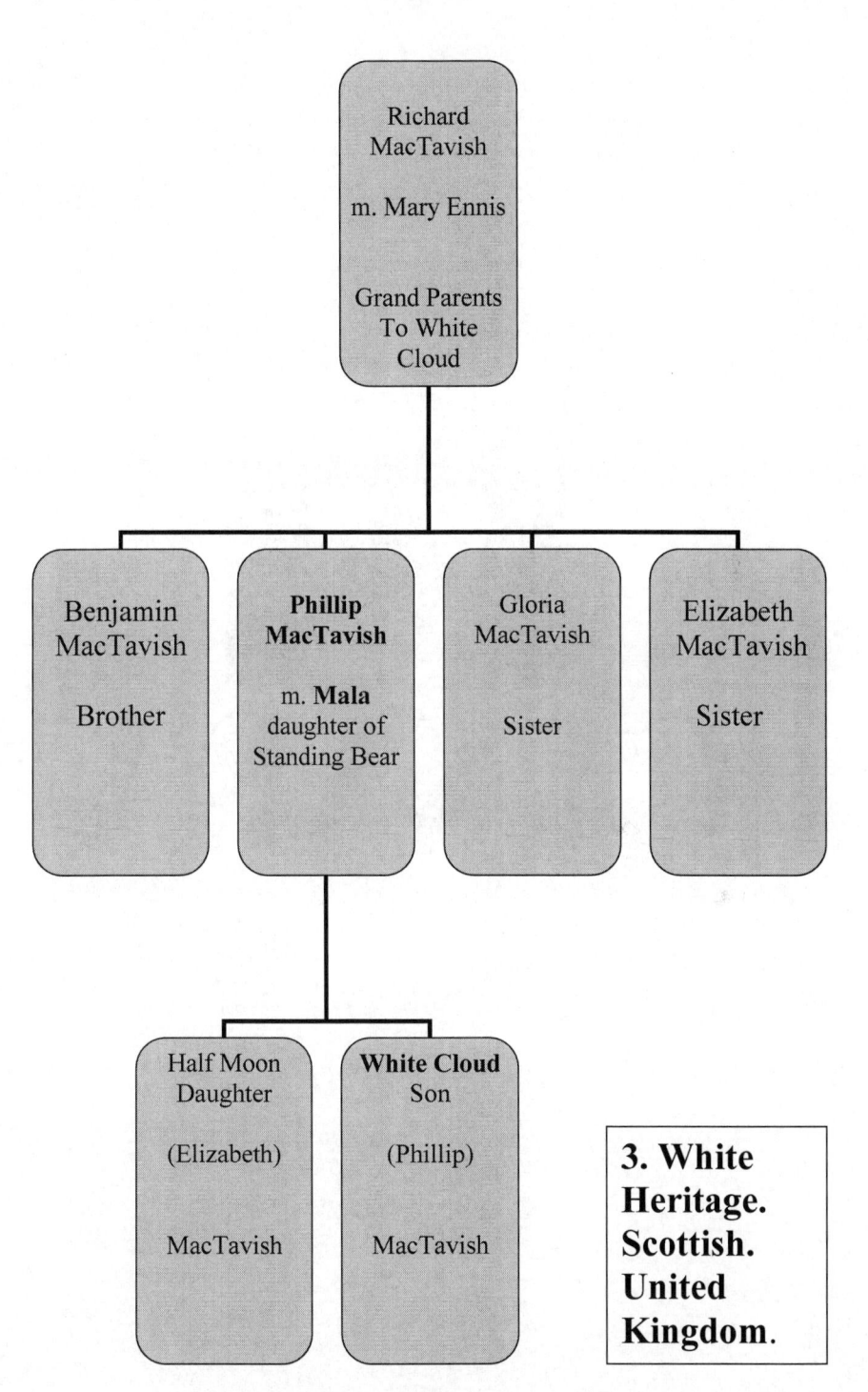

Moon Star

- **Richard MacTavish**
  m. Mary Ennis
  Grand Parents To White Cloud
  - Benjamin MacTavish — Brother
  - **Phillip MacTavish** — m. **Mala** daughter of Standing Bear
    - Half Moon Daughter (Elizabeth) MacTavish
    - **White Cloud** Son (Phillip) MacTavish
  - Gloria MacTavish — Sister
  - Elizabeth MacTavish — Sister

3. White Heritage. Scottish. United Kingdom.

87

Moon Star

CANADA